We Sang to your Tomatoes

An Ivy and Mack story

Written by Juliet Clare Bell

Illustrated by Gustavo Mazali

with Nuno Alexandre Vieira

Collins

Who and what is in this story?

Listen and say

Grandpa

Download the audio at www.collins.co.uk/839818

Grandpa's band

van

LEMON
BREAKFAST

Grandpa said, "Look at the lovely tomato plants in their new pots. They're growing."

Ivy said, "I know! They were very small!"

Mack said, "And now they're big. I love the flowers!"
Ivy said, "Me too."

Grandpa said, "Tomato plants like lots of water and lots of sun. Let's put them here."

Then Grandpa sang.

"Please grow, tomatoes. Grow, grow, grow.

Get big and red when I go, go, go!"

Mack said, "That's a silly song!"

Grandpa said, "I know. I like silly things!"

Ivy said, "Your van's here, Grandpa! I can see Sally from the band!"

Mack said, "I can see *everyone* from the band!"

Grandpa said, "Walk Banjo and water the tomato plants, please! See you soon!"

Bye-bye, Grandpa!

Ivy and Mack took Banjo for a walk and they watered the tomato plants every day.

Mack said, "I know! Grandpa sings to the tomato plants. Why don't we sing, too?"

Ivy said, "It's a silly song ... but I like it."

Mack said, "Me too."

The next day, the plants looked different.
Ivy said, "Look! Tomatoes!"
Mack said, "I can't see them."

Ivy said, "Look under the flowers. Small green tomatoes!"

Mack said, "Yes! I can see. It was our song! Let's sing to them every day!"

Ivy and Mack sang Grandpa's song to the tomatoes every day. After two weeks, the plants were bigger. But Ivy was sad.

Ivy said, "Why are the tomatoes small and green? Grandpa wanted big, red tomatoes."

On the way home, Ivy had an idea.

Dad said, "That's silly!"

Ivy said, "I know! Grandpa likes silly things!"

Dad said, "Me too!"

Ivy said, "Grandpa comes home today!"

Dad said, "Would you like to take Banjo to his house?"

Ivy said, "Yes, please!"

Mack said, "Yes, please! And we need *these*!"

At Grandpa's house, Ivy and Mack went to the tomato plants.

There was a noise outside.

Ivy said, "Quick! Grandpa's home!"

Ivy asked, "Are you happy to be home, Grandpa?"

Grandpa said, "Yes, I am. Are you here to help me?"

Mack said, "Yes! We walked Banjo and we sang to your tomatoes ..."

Ivy said, "And *look* at them!"

Grandpa said, "That's fantastic! Sing the song again!"

Picture dictionary

Listen and repeat

flowers

plant

pot

sun

tomatoes

water

1 Look and order the story

2 Listen and say

Collins

Published by Collins
An imprint of HarperCollins*Publishers*
Westerhill Road
Bishopbriggs
Glasgow
G64 2QT

HarperCollins*Publishers*
1st Floor, Watermarque Building
Ringsend Road
Dublin 4
Ireland

William Collins' dream of knowledge for all began with the publication of his first book in 1819.

A self-educated mill worker, he not only enriched millions of lives, but also founded a flourishing publishing house. Today, staying true to this spirit, Collins books are packed with inspiration, innovation and practical expertise. They place you at the centre of a world of possibility and give you exactly what you need to explore it.

© HarperCollins*Publishers* Limited 2020

10 9 8 7 6 5 4 3 2

ISBN 978-0-00-839818-7

Collins® and COBUILD® are registered trademarks of HarperCollins*Publishers* Limited

www.collins.co.uk/elt

British Library Cataloguing in Publication Data

A catalogue record for this publication is available from the British Library.

Author: Juliet Clare Bell
Lead illustrator: Gustavo Mazali (Beehive)
Copy illustrator: Nuno Alexandre Vieira (Beehive)
Series editor: Rebecca Adlard
Publishing manager: Lisa Todd
Product managers: Jennifer Hall and Caroline Green
In-house editor: Alma Puts Keren
Project manager: Emily Hooton
Editor: Deborah Friedland
Proofreaders: Natalie Murray and Michael Lamb
Cover designer: Kevin Robbins
Typesetter: 2Hoots Publishing Services Ltd
Audio produced by id audio, London
Reading guide author: Julie Penn
Production controller: Rachel Weaver
Printed and bound by: GPS Group, Slovenia

MIX
Paper from
responsible sources
FSC™ C007454

This book is produced from independently certified FSC™ paper to ensure responsible forest management.

For more information visit: **www.harpercollins.co.uk/green**

Download the audio for this book and a reading guide for parents and teachers at www.collins.co.uk/839818